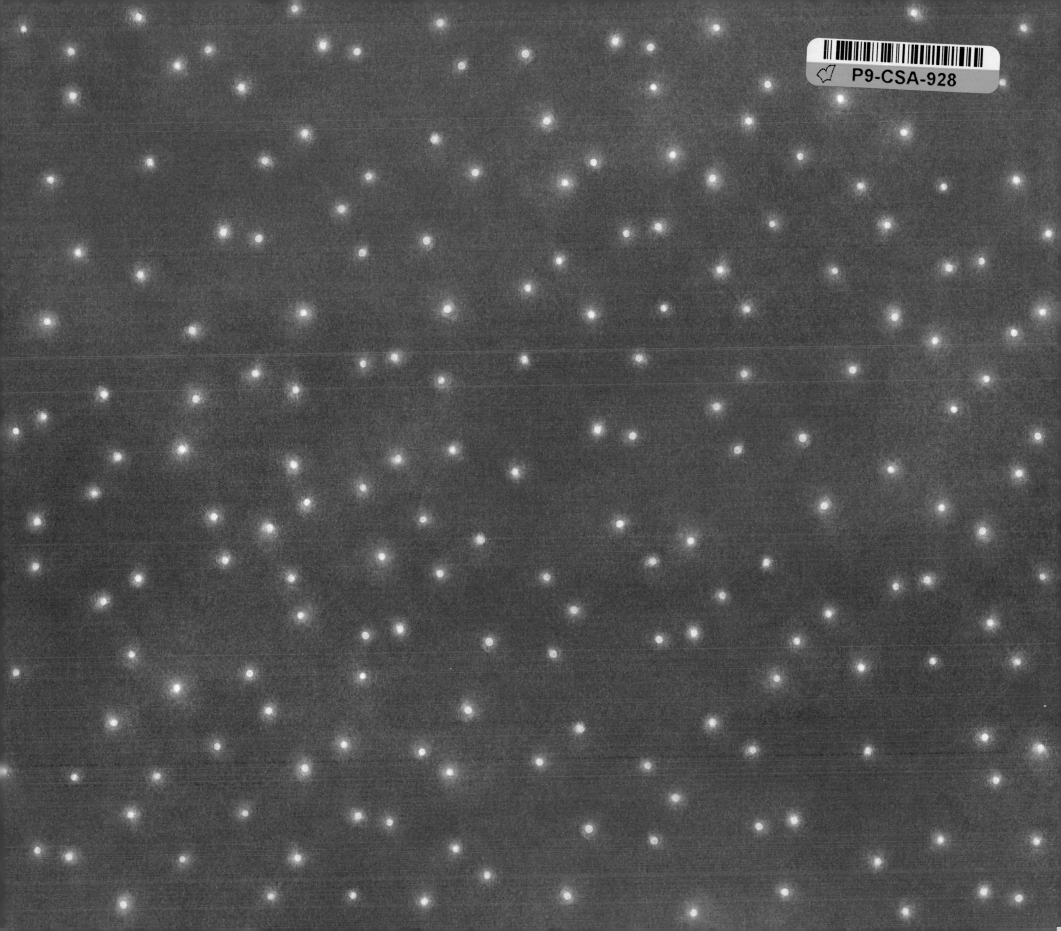

KINGS OF THE CASTLE

For Lucy

KINGS OF THE CASTLE

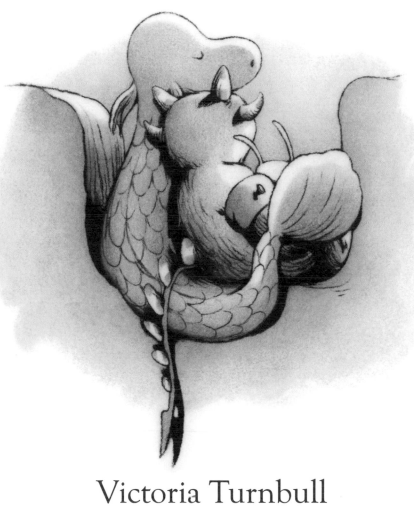

Victoria Turnbull

templar books
an imprint of Candlewick Press

George didn't want to waste
the night moonbathing.

He wanted to
build a sand castle

that would turn
any monster

green
with envy . . .

but Boris had other ideas.

Then, out of the sea . . .

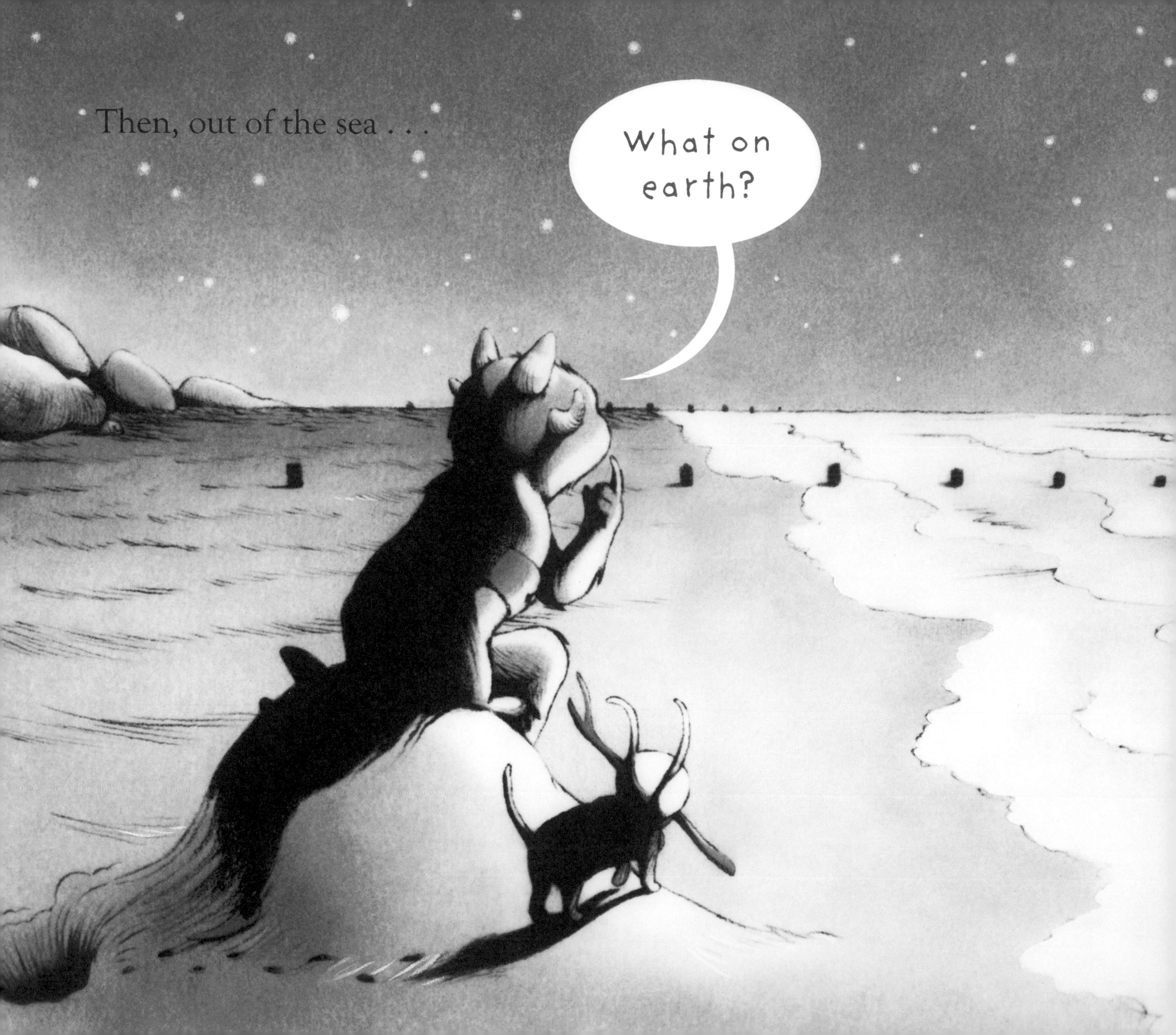

came the strangest-looking
creature George had ever seen.

George decided to introduce himself—the creature couldn't be worse company than Boris.

But

it

was

hopeless.

They

could

not

understand

one

another.

but Boris had other ideas.

Maybe they could be friends after all.

And so with a
little planning . . .

George and Nepo set to work.

And before long, the flag
could be raised.

They reigned until dawn.

George and Nepo
had done it.
They were now . . .

When the tide came in and the sun came up,

they headed for home.

The night was over . . .

but some things last forever.

First U.S. edition 2017

Library of Congress Catalog Card Number pending
ISBN 978-0-7636-9295-7

17 18 19 20 21 22 TLF 10 9 8 7 6 5 4 3 2 1

Printed in Dongguan, Guangdong, China.

This book was typeset in Goudy Old Style and Providence.
The illustrations were done in colored pencil.

TEMPLAR BOOKS

an imprint of
Candlewick Press
99 Dover Street
Somerville, Massachusetts 02144
www.candlewick.com

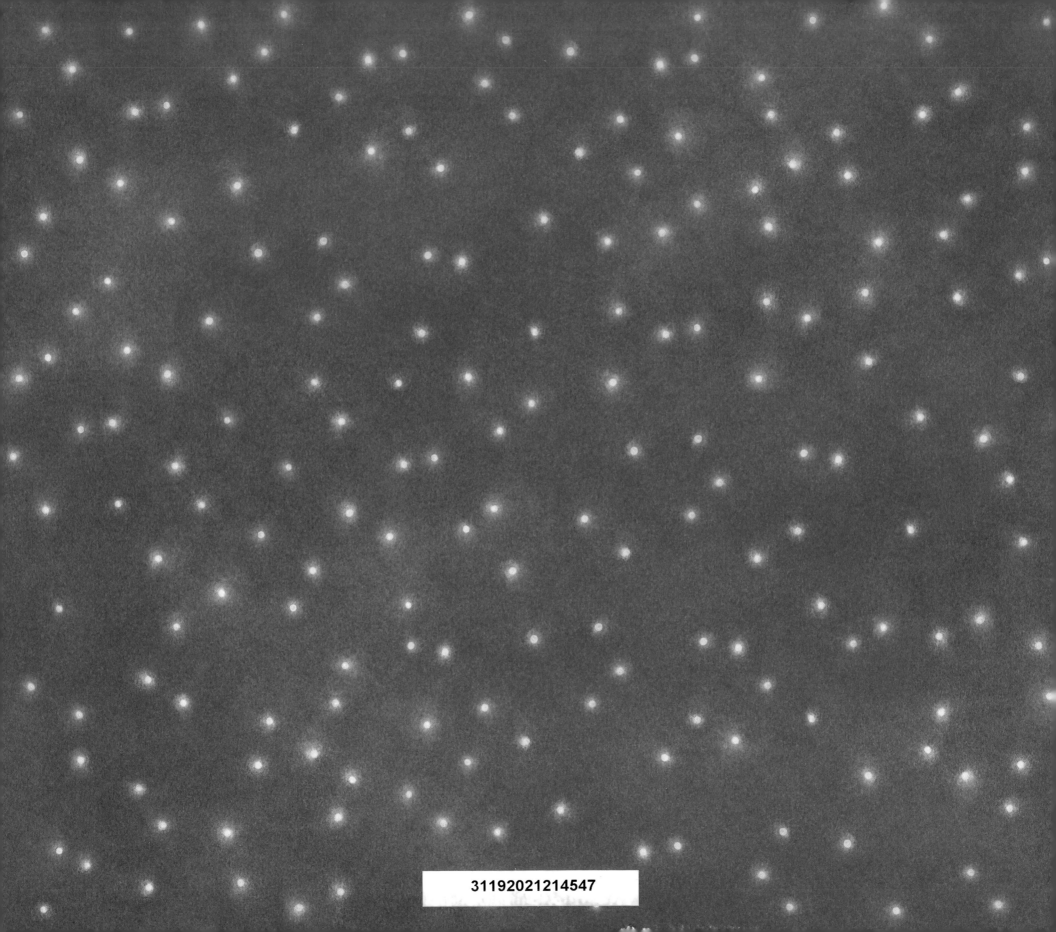

31192021214547